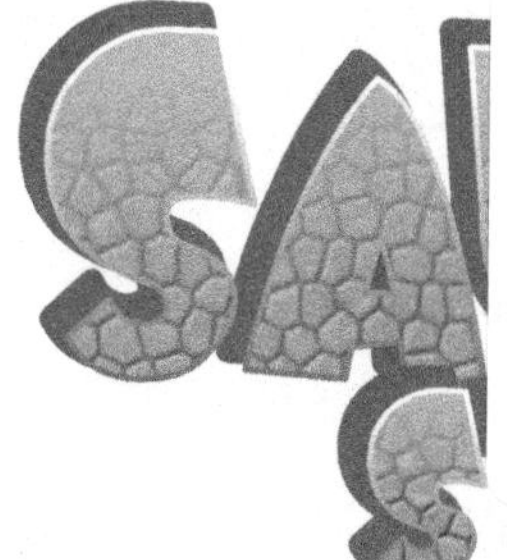

Tyrannosaurus in the Veggie Patch

SAURUS STREET

Tyrannosaurus in the Veggie Patch

Nick Falk and Tony Flowers

RANDOM HOUSE AUSTRALIA

For Jack and Louis, without whom there wouldn't be a Saurus Street
– Nick Falk

For Holly, without her dog walks on the beach, this book might never have been
– Tony Flowers

A Random House book
Published by Random House Australia Pty Ltd
Level 3, 100 Pacific Highway, North Sydney NSW 2060
www.randomhouse.com.au

First published by Random House Australia in 2013

Addresses for companies within the Random House Group can be found at www.randomhouse.com.au/offices

National Library of Australia
Cataloguing-in-Publication Entry

Author: Falk, Nicholas
Title: Tyrannosaurus in the veggie patch / Nick Falk; Tony Flowers, Illustrator
ISBN: 978 1 74275 655 4 (pbk)
Series: Falk, Nicholas. Saurus street; 1
Target Audience: For primary school age
Subjects: Tyrannosaurus – Juvenile fiction
Other Authors/Contributors: Flowers, Tony
Dewey Number: A823.4

Cover design by Leanne Beattie
Cover and internal illustrations by Tony Flowers
Internal design and typesetting by Anna Warren, Warren Ventures
Printed in Australia by Griffin Press, an accredited ISO AS/NZS 14001:2004 Environmental Management System printer

Random House Australia uses papers that are natural, renewable and recyclable products and made from wood grown in sustainable forests. The logging and manufacturing processes are expected to conform to the environmental regulations of the country of origin.

CHAPTER ONE
the veggie patch

That's weird. Charlie's not barking.

Why isn't she barking?

She always barks in the mornings.

Charlie's our dog. She's small and very **hairy**, and every single morning I get woken up by her barking to be let in. I don't blame her, really. Especially at this time of year. It's winter and it's really, really cold outside.

There's frost everywhere and some mornings there's even snow. I reckon Dad should let Charlie sleep inside in winter, but he won't. Sometimes, when Dad's not looking, I sneak outside and give her a few cushions from the sitting-room couch before I go to bed. And in the morning I sneak back out, get the cushions and put them back.

Sometimes they're a bit muddy but no-one seems to notice. I love Charlie. I reckon she's my best friend. Apart from Toby, of course. Toby lives next door. I've known him since forever.

Me and Toby as babies

But after Toby, Charlie's definitely number one.

Anyway, she's not barking and that's really **odd**.

I go outside and look for Charlie. She's not in her kennel. The two cushions I gave her aren't there either.

I look under the car. Nope. Not a dog in sight. She must be in the veggie patch. Charlie loves digging up Mum's vegetables.

I walk around the side of the house to look. But she's not there.

And that's really weird.

But not nearly as weird as what IS in the veggie patch.

There's a

GREAT BIG TYRANNOSAURUS.

It's lying right there in the middle of the veggie patch. I'm not kidding. It's enormous, with a huge head, huge feet and a massive tail.

I know it's a tyrannosaurus because I recognise the little arms with two claws from my dinosaur book.

My dinosaur book also says that tyrannosauruses are extinct. Which means they don't live anymore. And I can tell you one thing:

the book is wrong about that!

The tyrannosaurus opens one eye and looks at me. It looks guilty. And that doesn't surprise me. Because it's obviously eaten Charlie. And that makes me really mad. I'm just about to tell the dinosaur exactly what I think of it when

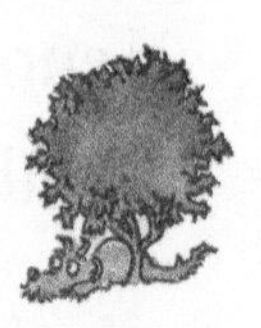

I hear a whining noise from behind me. I spin around and there's Charlie, hiding under a holly bush. She's not been eaten.

Hooray!

But she does look really scared, and that doesn't surprise me either.

Because there's a great big tyrannosaurus in the veggie patch!

Mum's gonna boil. That means she's gonna be really angry. I know

what it means because Dad once said he was 'boiling with rage' when I knocked into his new red car on my scooter and scratched the paintwork. And Mum's gonna be **REALLY** boiled about her vegetables.

- ☑ The cauliflowers are crushed.
- ☑ The green beans are goners.
- ☑ The tomatoes are toast.
- ☑ And the cabbages are kaput.

It's death by dinosaur for Mum's veggie patch.

I've got to get the tyrannosaurus out of here before Mum and Dad wake up.

You see, it's kind of my fault there's a tyrannosaurus in the veggie patch.

Last night I saw a shooting star outside my window, and I had to make a wish in a real hurry, because if you don't make a wish before the shooting star disappears it doesn't come true.

So I wished for the first thing I could think of that I really wanted. Which was a

real live tyrannosaurus.

And now here it is.

Guess I didn't think my wish through too well.

CHAPTER TWO
follow the leader

Before I do something about the tyrannosaurus, I need to find those cushions. Aunty Betty made those cushions and there'll be fireworks if I've gone and lost them.

I search the garden until I find a telltale cushion tassel lying on the lawn, right in front of the veggie patch.

I investigate further and it doesn't take me long to find another tassel.

It's sticking out from between the tyrannosaurus's teeth. No prizes for guessing what happened to the cushions then.

This tyrannosaurus is obviously hungry. Really hungry. Why else would he eat cushions? I need to find the tyrannosaurus some proper food. Or else he really will eat Charlie. Or me. **And neither option sounds good.** I tell him to stay put and I tiptoe inside to look in the fridge.

Steak.

That's what's in the fridge. Expensive steak. I unwrap it and put it on a plate. And for good measure I cover it with a good dollop of sauce. Then I go back outside.

Everything's still the same. The

tyrannosaurus is still lying in the veggie patch and Charlie's still hiding under the bush. The tyrannosaurus is looking hungrily at Charlie. I reckon he's decided she'll make a good dessert after those cushions. Looks like I've brought the steak in the nick of time.

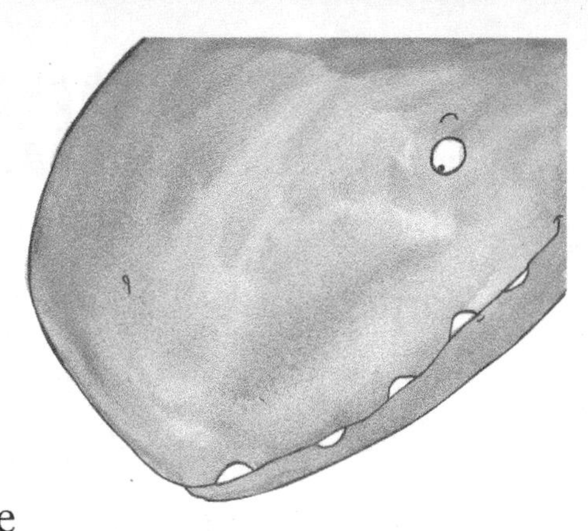

I hold the plate close to the tyrannosaurus's nose to let him get a sniff. Then I back off. I don't want to risk being gobbled up myself. But he's certainly caught the scent. He perks right up and is on his feet in a second.

He really is **enormous**.
He makes the big climbing tree in our garden look like a cricket stump. I'm not sure this steak's going to be enough.

I start to back away slowly and the tyrannosaurus follows me. His footsteps are really ***loud***.

Every step sounds like a lorry falling off a crane. And he's leaving massive footprints all over the place.

I need to hide him before Mum and Dad wake up.

Now, hiding a tyrannosaurus just isn't easy. It's not like hiding a comic or a chocolate bar. They're easy to hide. But a tyrannosaurus is way too big to hide under the bed or in the back of the sock drawer. I'm gonna need somewhere much, **much** bigger.

What about the garage? Nope. Dad's new car is in the garage and the tyrannosaurus is certain to SCRATCH it. He's got really big claws. I could try asking him not to touch the car, but I don't speak Dinosaur. And I don't think he speaks any English. I'm not sure English was even invented in the Cretaceous period (that's when tyrannosauruses lived – well, according to my dinosaur book, anyway).

I could try to **hide** him in my bedroom, I suppose. But I'm not sure he'd fit. And Mum would definitely notice him when she comes in with the vacuum cleaner. No. It's no good. I'm going to have to think of somewhere else.

CHAPTER THREE

my best friend

It's times like this when I need a bit of help, which is where my best friend Toby comes in. He's got glasses, which is a sure sign he's a genius.

Toby can solve any puzzle in the world. When he grows up, he's going to build a space rocket and fly to Jupiter. Jupiter's the biggest planet in the solar system, and it's made entirely out of gas.

I bet Toby can think of somewhere to hide my tyrannosaurus.

The dinosaur has still got its eyes on the steak. It looks

I back out of the garden gate. I leave it open so it can follow me. There was no need to, though. The tyrannosaurus just steps over the fence.

I start walking slowly towards Toby's house. I'm still walking backwards, keeping both my eyes on the tyrannosaurus. I'm almost at Toby's gate when I hear a door opening across the road.

Oh no.

It's Mrs Wilcott. Mrs Wilcott is

at least a hundred years old and I'm under strict orders not to give her another scare. Last week I almost knocked her over with my scooter and Mum said Mrs Wilcott almost jumped out of her skin. If she got that scared by my scooter, goodness knows what's gonna happen when she sees my tyrannosaurus.

Luckily she doesn't come outside. She's just opening the door to let her cat in. Good thing too. I bet tyrannosauruses like to eat cats. Sabre-toothed tigers are cats. And tyrannosauruses liked to eat them.

I open Toby's gate and creep up

to his window. I leave the steak on the pavement outside the gate. No need for the tyrannosaurus to destroy Toby's garden as well.

I watch as the tyrannosaurus gobbles up the steak in one big gulp. Hardly even a mouthful. He's still super hungry. I better hurry up.

I knock on Toby's bedroom window. No answer. I knock a bit louder. Still no answer. I put my ear to the window and listen. I can hear a grunting, snorting, roaring sound coming from inside Toby's room. But don't worry, there isn't a dinosaur in his room. It's just Toby **snoring**. He snores really loudly. I slept over at his house once and his snoring kept me awake all night.

I knock **louder**.

'Toby! Wake up!' I whisper. I don't want to wake up Toby's parents. Toby would be really angry if my tyrannosaurus ate his parents.

Toby opens the curtains and peers out. He hasn't got his glasses on. Toby can't see very well without his glasses.

'Who's that?' says Toby.

'It's me, Jack,' I say. 'I need your help to hide a big tyrannosaurus. I wished for a tyrannosaurus last night, and this morning I found him in the veggie patch.'

'I don't believe you,' says Toby.

'It's true,' I say. 'Come outside and I'll show you. But be quiet.'

'I'm not going anywhere,' says Toby. 'It's only six in the m–

AAARGH! WHAT'S THAT?!'

CHAPTER FOUR

the dinosaur whistle

Toby's face turns as **white** as paper. I'm wondering what's made him look like that when I feel warm air on my cheek.

I look to my left and there's the tyrannosaurus. His nose is right up against the window. He's come to see who I'm talking to. My face is right next to his teeth. Some of them are bigger than my head.

Toby's dressed and out the door in ten seconds flat. He's got his glasses on this time.

'That's So cool,' says Toby.

He's super impressed. Last week was Toby's birthday, and he got a new remote-controlled car. I was really jealous. But I reckon my tyrannosaurus totally beats his remote-controlled car.

'What are you going to do with him?' asks Toby.

'I need to hide him before Mum and Dad wake up. He's smashed all Mum's vegetables.'

'Where are you going to hide him?' asks Toby.

'I don't know,' I say. 'That's why I need your help. I need you to think of somewhere no-one will find him.'

Toby thinks. He furls his brow, purses his lips and curls his finger around his chin.

'I've got it!' Toby shouts. 'The old abandoned house! The one in the woods on the other side of the river! You could hide a diplodocus in there!'

Toby's right.

Why didn't I think of it before? The big old house in the woods. No-one's lived there for years. It's dark and **scary** and all the windows are broken. I've always been far too frightened to go near the place. But this is an **EMERGENCY**. So it looks as if I don't have a choice.

'Okay. Let's go,' I say. 'But how are we going to get him to follow us? I've run out of steak.'

'We could cover you in sauce and get him to chase you,' suggests Toby.

I don't like this idea much.

'Or, we could use my dinosaur whistle!'

'Your what?' I ask.

'My dinosaur whistle. My uncle sent it to me for my birthday. He lives in South America. It makes a **noise** that only dinosaurs can hear. Wait here. I'll go and get it.'

Now I'm really jealous. A remote-controlled car AND a dinosaur whistle! Time I started making a wish list for my next birthday.

'Here it is!' Toby's back. In his hand he's holding a red plastic whistle. It looks a bit like a dog whistle. The kind that makes a high-pitched noise

that people can't hear but makes dogs **GO CRAZY**.

I used one on Charlie once. She went bonkers and tried to bite me on the bottom.

'Are you sure that's not a dog whistle?' I ask.

'Yes. It's a dinosaur whistle,' says Toby. 'My uncle uses them all the time. He says South America is full of dinosaurs.'

I'm not sure that's true. South America has armadillos, which are covered in **armour**, and it has marmosets, which are a type of tiny monkey, and it has jaguars too, which are like leopards but with circles instead of spots. But I don't think it has dinosaurs.

No-one has dinosaurs anymore.

Except me. I've got a tyrannosaurus.

'C'mon. Let's try it,' says Toby.

So we tiptoe back out of the garden and into the road. The tyrannosaurus follows us. He's looking at me expectantly. I think he wants more steak. I hate to think what'll happen when he realises I haven't got any.

'Okay, here goes,' says Toby. And he blows as hard as he can on his dinosaur whistle.

Nothing happens.

Not at first anyway. The whistle doesn't make any noise at all. And the tyrannosaurus doesn't even notice. He just keeps staring at me, waiting for me to magic up more steak. But then, after a few seconds, a dog starts barking. And then another dog. And pretty soon all

the dogs in the road are barking. And it's **really, really loud**. And that's bad.

But not nearly as bad as what happens next.

Charlie comes running through the open gate of our garden. She looks pretty mad. I think my bottom may be in for another biting. But . . . oh no! It's not my bottom she's after.

IT'S THE DINOSAUR'S!

Charlie makes a beeline for the tyrannosaurus, jumps up and bites him on the tail.

The tyrannosaurus is not happy about being bitten. Not at all. He lets

out a mighty roar and starts running down the road.

SMASH!

He treads on Mr Johnson's car, crushing it like a tomato.

WHAM!

He knocks into a lamppost and breaks it like a twig.

CRASH!

He charges straight through Doris Codswallop's garden fence. Charlie's still chasing after him, biting at his heels.

Lights are coming on in houses

up and down the street. Everyone is starting to wake up. And I'm not surprised. It sounds as though an angry tyrannosaurus is running down the street. Which is, of course, precisely what it is.

Toby and I start racing down the road, doing our best to keep up with the rampaging dinosaur. 'What are we gonna do?' I gasp between breaths. I'm not used to running this *fast*.

'I could try my dinosaur whistle again?' says Toby.

'NO!' I quickly reply. 'Anything but that!'

'Well, what about this then?' And without waiting for an answer Toby puts his fingers between his lips and lets out the loudest whistle I've ever heard

in my life. I reckon it's loud enough to be heard on the moon.

All the dogs stop barking. The tyrannosaurus stops dead in his tracks. He spins around and starts trotting back towards us.

'Not bad, eh?' Toby smiles. 'Learnt that in the scouts. It's what you're supposed to do if you get lost.'

'Well, no-one's going to lose you in a hurry,' I say.

I'm pretty impressed.

'C'mon, let's get this tyrannosaurus hidden before someone spots us.'

CHAPTER FIVE
the abandoned house

We start running towards the woods. The tyrannosaurus is hot on our heels.

So is Charlie, who seems to have recovered from the dinosaur whistle. She's wagging her tail and seems to be enjoying herself.

The tyrannosaurus is the one looking **nervous**. He's keeping an eye on Charlie in case she tries to bite him again.

Just as we're reaching the edge of the woods I start to hear people coming outside to see what the ruckus is all about. They're not going to be pleased when they see the **mess** we've caused. Fortunately we disappear into the woods in the nick of time. I'll have to deal with that problem later.

The abandoned house is in the deepest, darkest part of the woods. First we cross the river, trying to keep to the rocks so we don't get our feet wet. I have to carry Charlie across. She's too small to jump.

It's no problem for the tyrannosaurus, though. He leaps across in a single bound. From there we head **deeper** and **deeper** into the gloom of the forest. Before long the trees are so tall that we can't see the sun. It's as black as night. All I can see of the tyrannosaurus is his eyes. They're bright green and shining like torch beams. Charlie's starting to whine again. She doesn't like the dark. I don't either. It's really scary.

I'm glad we've got a tyrannosaurus with us. I reckon if we saw any ogres or trolls the tyrannosaurus would just eat them.

Pretty soon we get to the abandoned house. It's much bigger than I remember. And much more **SPOOKY**. The front door

is half-open, the windows are broken and the curtains are flapping in the wind, like GHOSTS.

'How are we going to get the tyrannosaurus inside?' I whisper to Toby.

'Through the back doors. They're really big,' he answers.

'How do you know? Have you been here before?'

'Once,' says Toby, 'for a dare. I was really scared, though.'

We walk to the back of the house. The back doors are already wide open. I glance inside the house. For a few seconds I'm sure I can see something moving. But then I look again and there's nothing. I must have been imagining it.

'I hope the Bug Beast doesn't get us,' whispers Toby.

I freeze. 'The Bug Beast? Wh-what's that?'

'It's what got the people who lived here before,' says Toby. 'The Bug Beast came in the night and turned them into spiders.'

I stay frozen. 'What does it look like?'

'Nobody knows,' says Toby.

'Some say it's made of worms and centipedes. Some say it's made of eyeballs and toenails.' Toby's voice becomes very quiet. 'No-one knows, because no-one who's seen the Bug Beast has lived to tell the tale.'

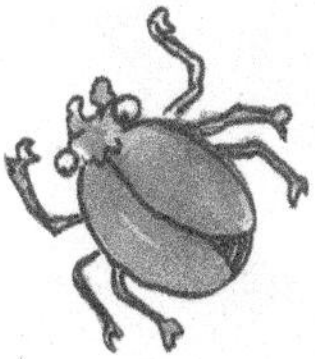

A shiver goes down my spine. 'Maybe this isn't such a good idea after all,' I whisper.

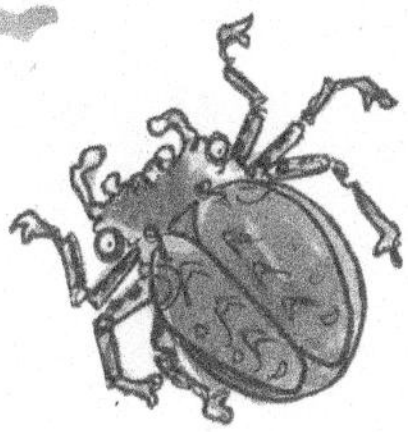

But the tyrannosaurus has other ideas. He suddenly sniffs the air and runs into the house. Clearly he can smell something.

I hope it's not the Bug Beast.

'Hey, where are you going?' I shout after him.

'C'mon,' says Toby, 'we better find out.'

We follow the tyrannosaurus into

the house. He doesn't quite fit through the door, and as he runs his head knocks a hole in the wall.

For a second I think the house is going to **fall down**. But it stays standing. Just. Once he's inside the house, the tyrannosaurus runs straight through another wall and then disappears around a corner.

'Wait!' I shout after him. We run through the hole he's made and around the corner.

The tyrannosaurus is in a dark room with no windows. I reckon it must be the **scariest** room in the whole house. He's standing in a corner and seems to be eating something. Hopefully it's the Bug Beast. I creep closer but it's so dark I can't see a thing.

Suddenly a light turns on behind me.

I almost *jump* out of my skin!

Just like Mrs Wilcott.

CHAPTER 6 frankfurters

It's Toby. Holding a torch.

'I got this when I went to get the dinosaur whistle.' He grins. 'I thought it might be helpful.' Toby shines the torch on the tyrannosaurus. He's not eating the Bug Beast. He's eating **frankfurters**. Lots and lots of frankfurters.

There must be about twenty packets of frankfurters hidden in a

wooden chest. Or what used to be a wooden chest. The tyrannosaurus has eaten that too.

'Teenagers,' says Toby.

My eyes widen.

'Are those frankfurters made of teenagers?' I say, turning white.

'No,' laughs Toby. 'Teenagers come here at night. To make a fire and tell ghost stories. Sometimes they bring frankfurters to cook.'

'Why?'

Toby shrugs. 'To scare off the Bug Beast, I suppose. I don't think the Bug Beast likes frankfurters.'

I think for a moment. 'Or maybe they bring frankfurters in case they get hungry?'

'Could be,' agrees Toby. 'Ghost stories always make me hungry.'

I look at the tyrannosaurus. He's already eaten all the frankfurters. Apart from one. Charlie managed to steal one while the dinosaur wasn't looking. She's lying under an old sink, chomping away on it. There's an old fridge in here as well. I think this room used to be the kitchen.

But what do we do now? Even after two **fat** steaks and twenty packets of frankfurters, the tyrannosaurus still looks hungry. He sure is greedy. He's started sniffing around the old fridge, but it doesn't look as if there's anything in there.

Toby's got his thinking face on again. That's good news. I need him to

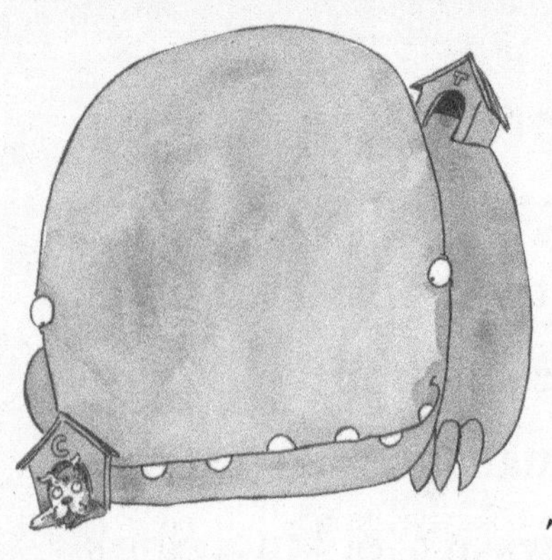

think of something really clever.

I know I can't keep my tyrannosaurus forever. There's no room in the garden to build him a kennel, and it'll cost way too much to feed him. And one day he'd be bound to eat someone. And then I'll be in loads of **trouble**. Unless it's Aunty Betty, of course. Mum and Dad might not be quite so angry if he eats Aunty Betty.

We need a clever idea. And if there's one thing Toby's great at, it's coming up with clever ideas.

'I've got it!' shouts Toby.

We all turn to him excitedly. Even the tyrannosaurus.

'We'll build a time machine and send the tyrannosaurus home!'

'Home? What do you mean, home?' I ask.

'Home! To dinosaur world!' says Toby.

'What? You mean the Cretaceous period?'

'That's the one. We'll send him back to the Cretaceous period!' Toby looks very pleased with his idea.

It's not a bad idea. I'm sure the tyrannosaurus

would love to go home. He must miss his family. And I'm sure he'd like a nice tender triceratops for lunch. Much tastier than **frankfurters**.

Toby stops to think. 'Time machines are made of two things,' he says. 'Time. And machines. So we need lots of time and lots of **MACHINES**.' He looks up, smiling. 'How many clocks do you have in your house?'

'Lots,' I answer. There are clocks all over our house. Dad always likes to know what time it is. He hates people being late. Even for breakfast.

'Right,' says Toby. 'You get the clocks. And I'll get the machines.'

'What about the tyrannosaurus?' I ask. Everyone in the street will be awake now. If we go back home with

the tyrannosaurus, everyone will know it was us who caused all the mess.

'Charlie can stay here and guard the tyrannosaurus,' says Toby confidently.

I'm not sure this is such a good idea. Charlie's too small to guard a tyrannosaurus.

But then Toby shines the torch

on the other side of the room. There's one more frankfurter left, hidden under some old newspapers. The tyrannosaurus is looking at it hungrily. But Charlie's **growling** at him and the tyrannosaurus is too scared to take it. How about that? The tyrannosaurus is scared of Charlie! Maybe that bite on the tail worked out better than I thought.

'But what about the Bug Beast?' I ask Toby.

'Don't worry. It only gets people. Charlie will be fine. So will the tyrannosaurus.'

I walk over to Charlie and give her a goodbye pat. 'Don't let that tyrannosaurus run away,' I say to her.

Charlie woofs in reply. Then

I go over and wave a finger at the tyrannosaurus.

'And you,' I say, 'stay here. And don't eat my dog. She's not a frankfurter.'

The tyrannosaurus rumbles in reply.

'C'mon,' says Toby. 'Let's go.'

CHAPTER 7

finding enough time

'You're late for breakfast,' says Dad.

It's the first thing he says when I get home. I look at the kitchen clock. It's two minutes past seven. Breakfast is usually at seven o'clock. I told you he was fussy about time.

'Why have you got **LEAVES** in your hair?' asks Dad.

I quickly feel my head. There really are leaves up there. Must be from the

forest. I think quickly. 'I've been playing outside. In Toby's garden.'

'What have you been doing? Rolling in leaves?'

'No.' I say. 'Just playing.' I feel bad lying to Dad. But I'm not sure he'd believe me if I told him about the tyrannosaurus.

'Well, just be careful,' says Dad. 'Something odd's been going on outside. Mr Johnson's car got crushed. And something smashed Doris Codswallop's fence.'

I try and look casual. 'Maybe it was a meteor,' I suggest.

'Could be,' says Dad. 'Or an escaped rhinoceros from the zoo. So be careful. Rhinos are really bad-tempered.

Especially when they're hungry.'

Dad hands me a shopping bag full of carrots. 'Here. Take these,' he says. 'Just in case. Rhinos love carrots.'

'Um . . . okay. Thanks, Dad.' I take the carrots and sit down to have breakfast. Toast today. With banana jam. Dad always buys really weird jams. He reckons they're **exotic**.

I look at the clock. It's a big round kitchen clock. Should be perfect for our time machine.

I need to find a way to get the clock down off the wall. It's pretty high, but I think I could reach it if I stood on the

table. But there's no way I can do that with Dad in the room.

'Hey, Dad,' I say, 'was that the doorbell?'

'I didn't hear anything,' says Dad through a mouthful of toast.

'There it is again,' I say. 'Someone definitely rang the doorbell.'

Dad looks up from his toast, 'Well, why don't you go and answer it then?'

I think quickly. 'Maybe it's someone from the zoo. With a picture of the escaped rhinoceros. They'll probably want to talk to an adult.'

Dad gets up. He looks **excited**. 'Maybe you're right,' he says. 'Good thinking.' He hurries towards the door. I probably should have told him he's got toast stuck to his cheek. But then there isn't really anyone at the door so no-one will notice.

I quickly *climb up* on the table and get the clock down off the wall. But where do I put it? Dad's on his way back. I need to think quickly. The carrot bag! I stuff the clock in *quickly*. I'm back in my chair just as Dad marches back into the kitchen.

'There wasn't anyone there,' he says. 'Are you sure you heard the doorbell?'

'Certain,' I say. 'Maybe they saw

the rhinoceros and had to run after it.'

That gets Dad going again. He's off to the front door to see if he can see any sign of the chase.

I think *fast*. There's another clock in the lounge room. I run in there, climb on the couch and pull it gently down off the wall. Then I run back to the kitchen and try and shove it in the bag. There are too many carrots in there. I take out a handful. But where can I hide them? The *flower* vase. Mum always puts fresh flowers in a vase on the kitchen table in the mornings.

I stuff the carrots into the vase and put the clock in the bag.

That's two clocks. But I don't think

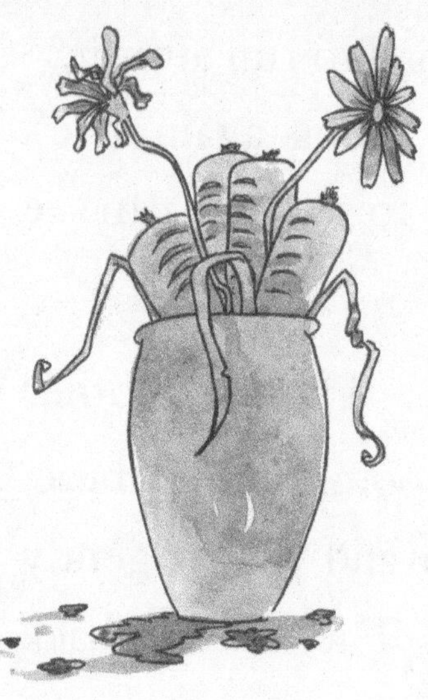

it will be enough. We're sending the tyrannosaurus all the way back to the Cretaceous period. The Cretaceous period was over 70 million years ago. That's a **l o n g , l o n g** time ago. So we're gonna need lots and lots of time to get him there. I'm going to need more clocks.

Dad's still outside, looking for the rhinoceros. I quickly finish my toast and go into my bedroom. I've got a plastic dinosaur clock next to my bed. It's only small, but I'm sure it'll help. Next I go upstairs to Dad's office. He's got an old DIGITAL watch on his desk. He doesn't wear it because the strap's broken.

That's four clocks. I'm still not sure that's enough. But there's only one clock left in the house. And that's in the most dangerous place in the whole universe.

CHAPTER 8

my sister's bedroom

My sister is a teenager, and a scary one. If she were a dinosaur, she'd be a velociraptor. Or maybe an allosaurus. One that can run really fast with really **SHARP CLAWS** and a **nasty bite**.

And right now my sister is asleep. In bed. In her room. And that makes her especially scary.

There's only one thing more dangerous than going into my sister's room. And that's going into my sister's room *when she's asleep*. Even Dad doesn't dare do that. But if I'm going to send my tyrannosaurus back to the Cretaceous period, I'll have to do it. I need that clock.

I sneak down the passage, and put my ear to my sister's door.

Silence.

Ever so slowly I push open the door. It's pitch black. The curtains are still closed. The only light is coming from her super cool glow-in-the-dark clock. I tiptoe into the room, one footstep at a time. I get closer. And closer. And **closer**. And just as I'm about to reach the clock I tread on something. It's her mobile

phone. It doesn't like being trodden on. It makes a loud **BEEPING** noise. My sister sits up in her bed.

'Who's in my room?' she roars.

My life flashes before my eyes. I need to get out of here before she sees me. I grab the clock, stuff it in the carrot bag, and run for my life.

'Jack? Is that you?' **growls** my sister as I escape through the door.

I don't say anything. If she catches me I'm as good as dead. I race back down the passage and tumble through the front door.

Dad's still out there looking for the phantom rhino.

'Where are you off to in such a hurry?' he says.

'I'm off to build a time machine,' I say, running past him.

Dad nods his head seriously. Clearly he knows all about time machines. 'Have you got the carrots?' he shouts after me.

'Got 'em,' I shout back, showing him the bag.

'Okay. Watch out for that rhino!'

I sprint out of the front gate. Toby's waiting for me. He's got a big bag with him as well. Full of machines, I reckon.

'What happened?' says Toby. 'You look as **white** as a sheet.'

'My sister,' I reply.

'Ooh, **scary**,' says Toby. He knows all about my sister. 'Well, let's go and send your tyrannosaurus home,' he says.

'Back to the Cretaceous!' I cry.

'Back to the Cretaceous!' shouts Toby, and we run back into the forest.

CHAPTER 9

time + machine = time machine

When we get back to the abandoned house Charlie and the tyrannosaurus are playing together.

I can hardly believe it.

The tyrannosaurus has chewed the leg off an old table, and he's throwing it for Charlie to fetch. And Charlie's trying to fetch it, but the table leg is a bit big for her. She can't get her mouth around it.

It's good to see them *playing*, though. I was really worried Charlie might get eaten.

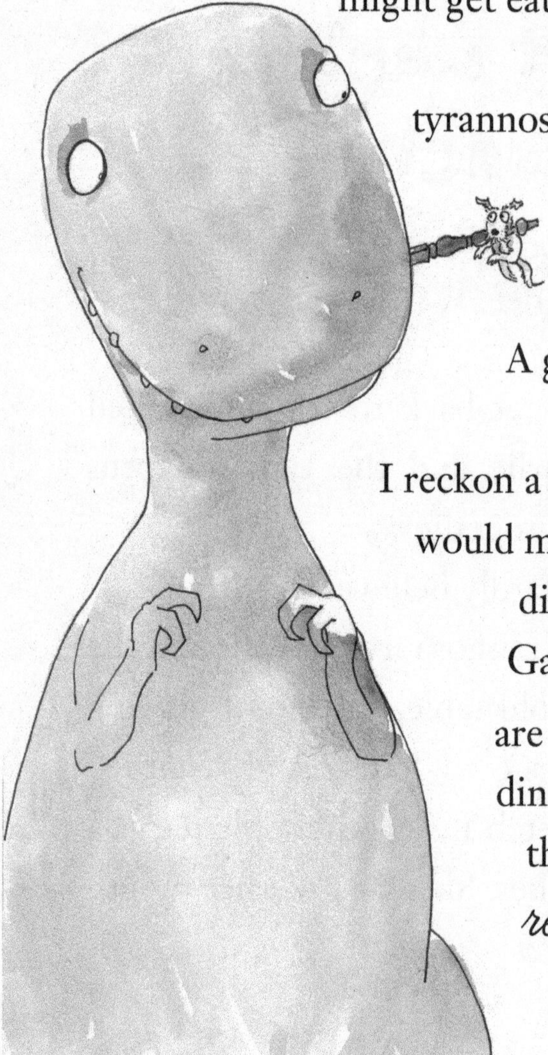

Maybe the tyrannosaurus plays with a pet back home?

A gallimimus, perhaps.

I reckon a gallimimus would make a great dinosaur pet.

Gallimimuses are **tall, thin** dinosaurs, and they can run *really fast* (that's what it says in my dinosaur book anyway).

I bet they'd be great fun to take for walks. Imagine going to the park with a pet gallimimus! All the other kids would be so jealous.

'C'mon,' says Toby. 'Let's build our time machine.'

We go into the old kitchen. Toby opens his bag. He takes out an **extra big** toaster, his remote-controlled car, a battery-operated robot claw and a calculator. A great selection of machines.

I open my bag and take out the digital watch and the four clocks.

'Now what do we do?' I ask.

'Simple,' says Toby. 'We connect the clocks and machines together.' He

takes a *roll of wire* from his pocket.

We set the alarms on all the clocks to go off in five minutes. Then we put the clocks in the toaster, put the remote-controlled car on top, and wrap everything together with *wire* so it can't move. Last of all we use the robot claw to hold everything in place.

'So, where are we sending him? The Jurassic period?' asks Toby.

'No', I say, 'the Jurassic's too long ago. Tyrannosauruses lived in the Cretaceous period.'

Toby hands me a piece of paper and a pencil. 'You should draw a map,' he says. 'We don't want to get lost.'

I carefully draw a timeline on the paper.

TRIASSIC PERIOD

↓

JURASSIC PERIOD

↓

CRETACEOUS PERIOD

All part of the Mesozoic Era. The time of the dinosaurs. Toby takes the map and tucks it under the wire.

'So,' says Toby. 'How long ago was the Cretaceous period?'

'About 70 million years,' I say.

'Perfect,' says Toby. He takes the calculator and types in -70 million. That's a minus sign, because we're going backwards, and then a 7 with seven zeros after it. Then he uses some wire to tie the calculator to the time machine.

'Now what?' I ask.

'Well,' says Toby, 'we only want the time machine to work on the tyrannosaurus, so we need a **magic** circle.'

He takes a stick of chalk from his pocket, and draws a huge circle on the floor. Then he puts the time machine in the middle.

'There' he says. 'Now only things inside the **magic** circle will go back in time.'

'How does that work?' I ask. 'You've just drawn a line.'

'Ah yes.' Toby smiles. 'But it's a **magic** line. Because this is **magic** chalk.'

'No it isn't. It's just ordinary chalk.'

'It most certainly is not,' says Toby. 'It's **magic** chalk. Look.' He passes me the box.

And there it is. '**MAGIC CHALK**.' Written in big silver letters on the side.

'Wow. That's so cool,' I say. 'When did you get that?'

Toby shrugs his shoulders. 'For my birthday, of course.'

I can't BELIEVE it. A remote-controlled car, a dinosaur whistle AND **magic chalk**! Toby gets the best birthday presents ever! It's so unfair.

CHAPTER 10

the bug beast

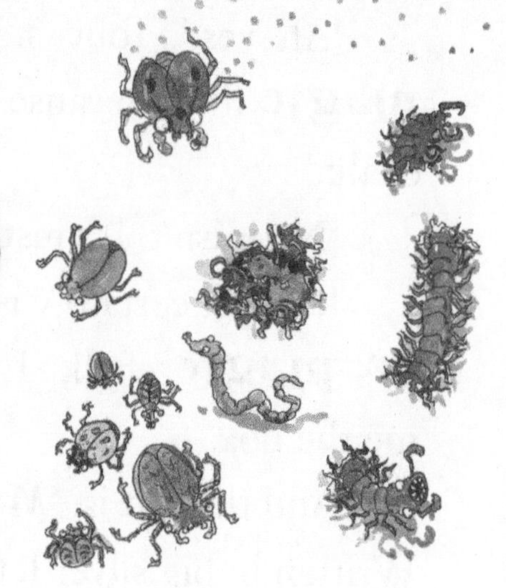

'Right,' says Toby, not even noticing me turning green with envy. 'Now all we have to do is get the tyrannosaurus into the circle. I reckon these should do the trick.'

He pulls a packet of sausages out of his bag and puts them in the middle of the **magic circle**, right next to the time machine.

It does the trick, all right.

The tyrannosaurus gets a whiff and runs straight into the circle. Charlie tries to follow, but I grab her collar to stop her.

'You should stay here, Charlie,' I say. 'I'm not sure you'd enjoy the Cretaceous period. It's not a place for dogs.' And that's true. Even the herbivores (which means plant eaters) were pretty FEROCIOUS in the Cretaceous period. There were triceratops, which had sharp, pointy horns and ankylosauruses, which had heavy clubbed tails, and even pachycephalosauruses, which had HARD bony heads and went around headbutting everyone. Charlie wouldn't last five minutes.

She still looks a bit sad, though. She doesn't want her new friend to go home. I feel sad too. I liked having a tyrannosaurus, even if he was a bit **scary**. But he can't stay.

Charlie, Toby and I watch the tyrannosaurus eat the sausages. He certainly looks as though he's enjoying them. He's making funny growly snuffling noises. It sounds a bit like Charlie eating dog food.

Then suddenly something amazing happens! The alarms on all the clocks go off at once. The tyrannosaurus lifts his head. He looks a bit surprised. But it's too late for him to run. Because the chalk line is glowing red, and there's a big red bubble around the time machine and the tyrannosaurus. And

then a jet of blue flame **shoots** out of the time machine. And then a red flame bursts out. And then the whole machine starts sparkling and shining. It looks as if it's filled with stars. And then there's a big **BOOM** and white light explodes out of the time machine. The red bubble is filled with crackling lightning. It's beautiful!

And then the tyrannosaurus, ever so slowly, starts to **fade**. It's as though he's turning see-through, like a window.

Suddenly Toby shouts, 'Holey-moley. What's that?'

'I know,' I shout back, thinking he's talking about the time machine. 'Isn't it amazing!'

'No, not that,' shouts Toby. 'THAT!' He points behind us. I spin around. Something **black** and **shadowy** is slinking across the floor towards us. It's so black I can hardly make out what shape it is. And then I see its eyes. They're bright green. And they look mean. And scary. Really, really scary.

'Oh no! It's the

BUG BEAST!'

I've never been more terrified in my life. I pick up Charlie and run as fast as I can away from the Bug Beast. But it's coming towards us. Getting closer and closer. And it's almost reached us! And that's when I see it more clearly . . . and . . .

Hang on. That's not a Bug Beast.

'It's just a stray cat,' gasps Toby, who's standing right next to me.

'Phew,' I sigh. 'Thank heavens for that.'

'Oh no!' gasps Toby.

I roll my eyes. 'What is it this time?' I ask.

'Look where we are!' shouts Toby.

I look around. But I can't see much. It looks as if I'm surrounded by glittering lights. Maybe I hit my head somewhere. And everything looks like it's coloured red.

And what's that? The tyrannosaurus. He's standing right next to me. Oh no . . . we can't be, but yes, we are!

We're inside the magic circle!

'We need to get out of here!' I shout.

But it's too late.

The house around us begins to disappear. And suddenly we're in a

spinning tunnel of colours and lights. And it feels like we're falling. We ARE *falling!* Down and down we go.

I cling on to Charlie and close my eyes. We're falling faster and faster. The wind is whistling through my ears.

We're gonna hit the ground . . . any . . . moment . . . now . . . and . . .

WHAM!

We land on soft green grass. I open my eyes. I'm on the side of a hill looking over an enormous valley.

There's a deep blue lake and trees that reach almost to the sky. There's a blood-red sun burning above the clouds. And down in the valley below me there are lots of animals. Big animals.

Really big animals.

'Dinosaurs,' whispers Toby. 'They're dinosaurs.'

We sit there, frozen. Nobody speaks. There's only one possible place we can be.

We've gone back to the Cretaceous period. We're in dinosaur world!

CHAPTER 11
meet the dinosaurs

'Well, what do we do now?' I ask Toby.

Toby shrugs. 'I don't know.'

'Do you think we should go back? Back to people world?'

'We can't,' says Toby. 'Look.' He's holding the time machine.

'Great,' I say. 'We've still got it!'

'Yes,' says Toby, 'but none of the machines are working. Watch.' He presses a button on the Robot

Claw. Nothing happens. The remote-controlled car isn't working either. 'The batteries must be used up,' says Toby.

'At least the calculator's still working,' I say. The screen is still lit up. But it doesn't say minus seventy million anymore. Now it just says zero. I guess it's because we've arrived.

'The calculator's no use without the other machines, though,' says Toby.

'A time machine needs machines to make it work. Time's no use on its own. That's why it's called a time *machine*.'

'Well, it seems as if we're stuck here,' I say.

I look around. It certainly is an amazing place.

Everything is **big**.

The trees are **big**.

The plants are **big**.

Even the grass is **big**.

It's growing so high it's almost over my head. And the dinosaurs look enormous. There are lots of them down at the bottom of the hill near the lake.

There aren't any diplodocuses or apatosauruses. They lived in the Jurassic period, which was even longer ago. But I can see some triceratops,

and some parasaurolophuses, and even some giant muttaburrasauruses. And flying in the sky there are some gigantic pterodactyls. It's pretty exciting. A bit scary, though. I'm glad we've got a tyrannosaurus to protect us.

'Hey, where are you going?' shouts Toby.

I spin around just in time to see our tyrannosaurus running off down the hill. He's running straight towards a herd of triceratops. I knew they'd be his **favourite** food. The triceratops see him coming, though. One of them makes a really deep *looooowing* sound, alerting his friends. And off they run, with our tyrannosaurus *snapping* at their heels.

It looks as if we don't have a tyrannosaurus to protect us after all. Now we really are in trouble.

'C'mon,' I say, 'we better find somewhere safe to hide. There might be other carnivores nearby.'

Toby doesn't like the sound of that. Neither does Charlie. They both look at me **nervously**. We start making our way down the hill, making sure we move as quietly as we can.

'What kind of carnivores are there in the Cretaceous period?' whispers Toby.

We're getting closer and closer to the lake, crouching **low** so we're hidden by the giant grass. Charlie's walking in front, **sniffing** the air to scout for danger.

'Well, there's the tyrannosaurus, of course,' I whisper.

'Right,' Toby whispers back, peering through the grass at a prowling spinosaurus. 'What else?'

'Those,' I say, indicating the spinosaurus. 'Those are meat eaters.'

Toby ducks his head down super fast.

'But they only eat fish.'

Toby relaxes again.

'And then there's the carnotaurus,' I add.

'Carnosaurus, you mean,' says Toby, as we carefully tiptoe around a dozing ankylosaurus.

'No. Carnotaurus,' I say.

'What are they like?' asks Toby. 'Nice and little?'

'No, they're **huge**, with two big horns on their head, and they can eat like a hundred roast chickens in one mouthful.'

'Great,' says Toby. 'I'm only about twenty roast chickens. That makes me less than a quarter of a mouthful.'

'And of course there are velociraptors,' I whisper, as we creep behind a grazing brachiosaurus.

'You mean the really fast ones with RAZOR SHARP claws?' asks Toby with a gulp.

'Yes. That's them,' I whisper. Wow. This brachiosaurus really is enormous. His head is almost touching the clouds.

'Well, now I'm **petrified**,' says Toby. 'You can't get much scarier than a velociraptor.' He looks scared. Charlie looks pretty worried too. I've never seen her so quiet. Even her snuffling is almost silent.

'I'm afraid you can get scarier than that,' I say, 'because the Cretaceous period was also home to the biggest meat-eating dinosaur that ever lived. The giganotosaurus.'

'Now you're just making things up,' whispers Toby.

''Fraid not,' I say. 'Giganotosauruses are even bigger than tyrannosauruses. And meaner too.'

Toby's turning **whiter** by the second. 'Well, let's hope we don't bump into one of those,' he says.

I couldn't agree more.

We've almost reached the lake. There's an incredible number of dinosaurs gathered around the water, taking a drink.

It really is amazing. I peer over the top of the grass to try to get a better look. I can see even more types of dinosaur now. Lumbering iguanodons with long, pointy thumbs and grumbling protoceratops with hard, bony crests. I take a couple of steps closer, to get a better look . . . and . . .

SWOOP!

What was that?

CHAPTER 12
the flying assassin

'Quick! Duck!' shouts Toby, pulling me back into the long grass. Charlie's pulling me back too, teeth clamped onto the heel of my shoe.

I look up. It's a **huge** pterodactyl. It tried to grab me with its claws. It's hovering above us now, looking for a way to snatch us out of the grass.

'What does it want?' says Toby, lying face down on the ground.

'I think it wants to **eat** us,' I say, 'or maybe take us to its nest as food for its children.'

Toby shudders. 'I don't like the sound of that at all,' he says. 'When I got out of bed this morning to help hide your tyrannosaurus, I did not expect to end up as breakfast for a baby pterodactyl.'

We stay as still as we can. Eventually the pterodactyl gives up and flies away.

'We need to get to somewhere safe,' says Toby.

We stand up slowly . . .

'Look. Over there,' I say. 'There's a cave in the side of that mountain.'

Toby peeks over the top of the grass. 'Looks good,' he says. 'Let's make a run for it.'

We wait a moment, just in case there's danger. Charlie sniffs the air. Then she sniffs again. And then she gives one quick wag of the tail. That's our secret signal. The coast is clear.

'Let's go,' I say.

We start running as fast as we can away from the lake and towards the cave. A couple of triceratops turn to look at us, but fortunately they don't seem very interested. We're going to make it. We get closer . . . and closer . . . and then suddenly I sense a shadow passing in front of the sun. Is it a cloud? I look up.

'THE PTERODACTYL,' screams Toby. 'IT'S BACK!'

The enormous winged reptile is swooping down towards me, its curved claws ready to snatch. I keep running as fast as I can. But I'm not sure I'm going to make it. I look up again. The pterodactyl is right above me. I close my eyes.

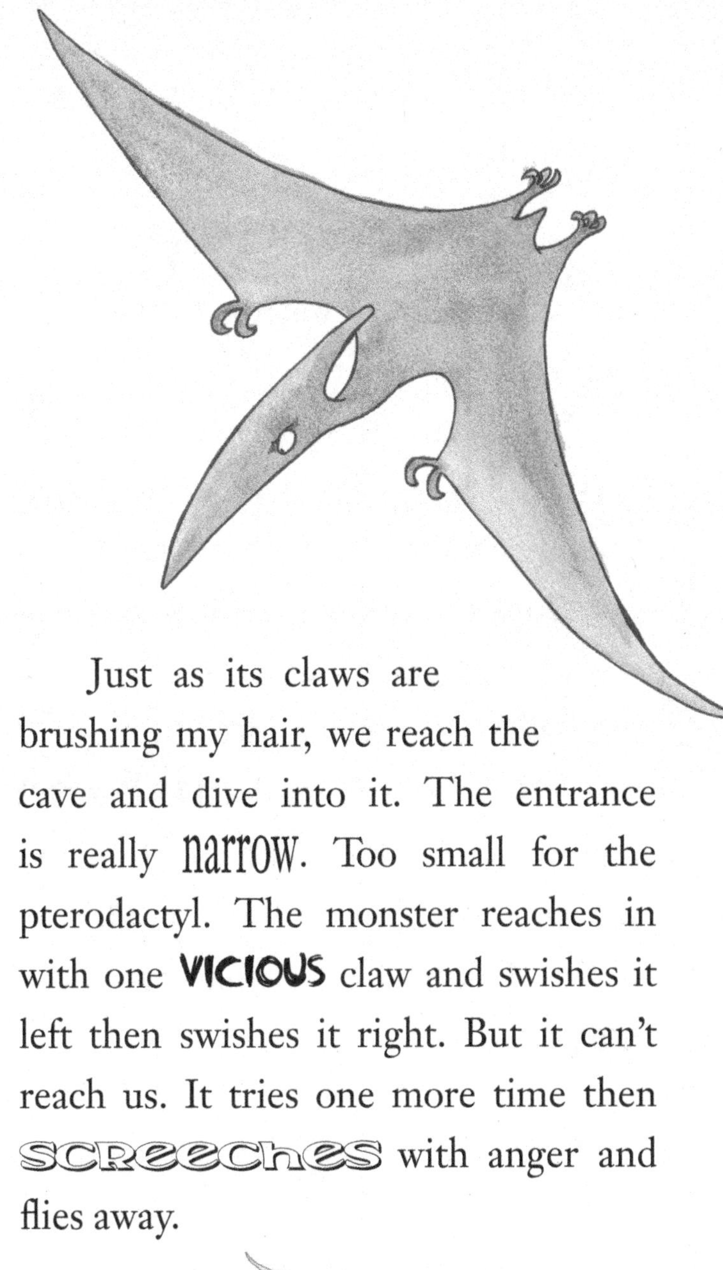

Just as its claws are brushing my hair, we reach the cave and dive into it. The entrance is really narrow. Too small for the pterodactyl. The monster reaches in with one **VICIOUS** claw and swishes it left then swishes it right. But it can't reach us. It tries one more time then SCREECHES with anger and flies away.

'Whoa,' says Toby. 'That was close.'

'Really close,' I say.

I feel pretty **shaky**. I can't believe how close I was to ending up as a dino snack.

Charlie nuzzles my neck to check I'm okay. I put my arm around her. A doggy cuddle is just what I need.

I look out of the cave. It seems as if it's starting to rain.

'What we need,' says Toby, 'is a plan.' He's inspecting the **broken** time machine. He's got his thinking face on again. Then all of a sudden he smiles. 'I think I might have an idea,' he says.

CHAPTER 13
storm power

'If we're going to get home,' says Toby, 'we need to get this time machine working again.'

'But it's **broken**,' I say. 'The machines aren't working anymore. You said so.'

'Yes,' says Toby, getting more and more excited, 'but that's just because they've run out of electricity.'

I'm confused. So is Charlie. We both give Toby a puzzled look.

'Look,' says Toby, 'machines need **electricity** to work, right?'

Charlie and I nod our agreement.

'And on the way here the electricity came from the batteries, yes?'

'Okay,' I say.

'So all we need to get us home is more electricity.'

I'm confused again. 'I thought you said the batteries were dead?'

'They are,' says Toby, 'but batteries aren't the only place you get electricity from. Where else can you get electricity?'

Charlie and I look at each other. Charlie shrugs. 'Well . . .' I say, 'from power points, I suppose. But I don't

think power points were invented in the Cretaceous period.'

'Of course they weren't,' says Toby, hopping from foot to foot with excitement. 'But there's something else that can give us electricity.'

Toby points at the rain outside. '*Lightning!*' he says. 'What we need is lightning! Lightning is the best source of electricity in the world!'

Now I'm excited too. 'And if there's

rain, there might be lightning too!'

'Not just might be. Definitely,' says Toby. 'Listen!'

I listen. And then I hear it. A huge rumble of **thunder**. The sound of lightning crackling across the sky!

Toby looks very pleased with himself. But there's one small problem.

'If we're going to find lightning,' I say, 'we need to go back outside.'

'That's right,' says Toby.

'And the pterodactyl is outside,' I say.

'Yes,' agrees Toby.

'And if we go outside, that pterodactyl might come back and eat us.'

Toby thinks for a second. 'Well, that's true,' he says, 'but I don't really think we have a choice.'

Hmmm . . . unfortunately he's right. We don't have a choice. We're going to have to risk it.

I kneel down and give Charlie a pat on the head. 'Are you ready, Charlie?'

Charlie woofs.

'Okay,' I say to Toby. 'Let's do it.'

Ever so quietly we tiptoe back out of the narrow cave entrance. I look up at the sky. I can't see any sign of the pterodactyl. And I can't see any other dinosaurs either. And I'm not surprised. There's a dinosaur-sized storm outside. The rain is coming down in buckets. Each droplet is enormous, like having a cup of water emptied over your head. In less than a second I'm drenched.

Another huge growl of thunder

rolls across the clouds. And then a flash of white hot lightning splits the sky. It almost touches the top of the mountain above us.

'C'mon,' says Toby, 'we need to get to the mountain peak. That's where the lightning's going to *strike*.'

We start climbing. At first we're climbing through forest. The trees are covered in thorns that tear my clothes. But we keep going, keeping our eyes to the ground to shield them from the rain.

Pretty soon we come to the edge of the forest, and the mountainside turns into bare barren rock. It's **volcanic** rock, black with sharp edges. I can feel it cutting through the bottom of my shoes.

Charlie starts to whine a little. The

sharp volcanic rock must be hurting her paws. But we're getting closer. The mountain peak is just above us.

'We're going to make it!' shouts Toby triumphantly.

But then we hear a sound. A low rumbling **growl**. We stop dead in our tracks.

'W . . . w . . . was that more thunder?' says Toby.

I shake my head. It didn't sound like thunder.

And then we hear a footstep. A great big stomp that makes the ground shake.

'M . . . m . . . maybe it's a b . . . b . . . big b . . . b . . . brachiosaurus,' croaks Toby.

I don't think so. I've got a feeling it's something **much scarier** than a brachiosaurus.

'Oh no,' whispers Toby. 'There it is!'

CHAPTER 14

the great escape

I look up. A head is starting to appear around the corner in front of us. A **big** head. A **very big** head. A very big head with a very big mouth. And that mouth is filled with **very, very big** teeth. The head is attached to a body that's bigger than a house, with two small arms and two enormous legs, each with three clawed toes. It's the biggest, **scariest** dinosaur imaginable.

'Is that what I think it is?' says Toby in a very small voice.

'I'm afraid so,' I whisper back.

It's a **giganotosaurus**.

The giganotosaurus sees us. It opens its mouth as **wide** as it can and lets out a deafening roar. And then it starts to charge.

'RUN!' I scream. We turn and sprint back down the mountain. But it's no good. In ten seconds the giganotosaurus has caught up with us.

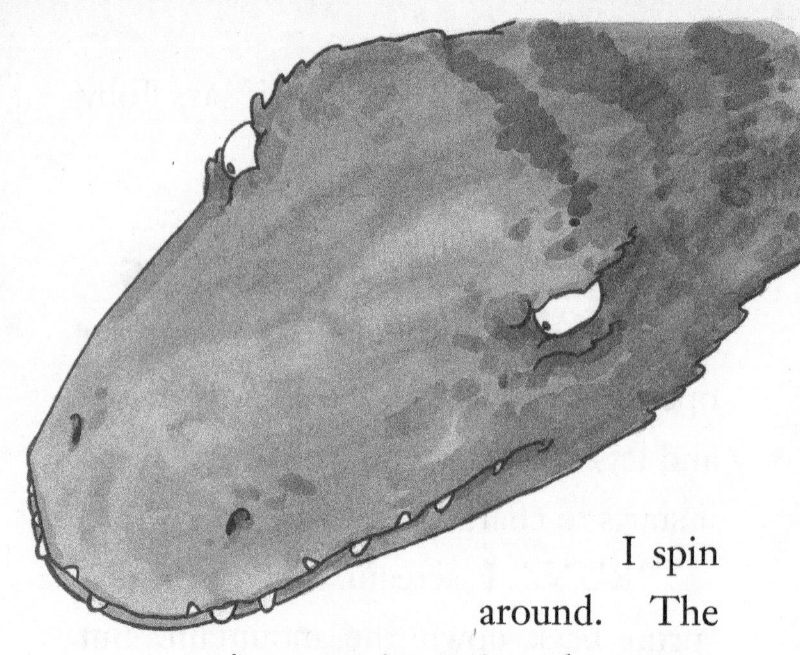

I spin around. The giant carnivore is only metres away. There's **no escape**. This time we really are going to get eaten. I curl up into a ball and cuddle Charlie under my body. Toby curls up next to me.

'Goodbye Jack,' whispers Toby.

'Goodbye Toby,' I whisper back.

Charlie lets out a little whimper.

The giganotosaurus **roars** again, and then lowers its head to eat

us. I screw my eyes up tightly and hold my breath. I hope it's over quickly.

And that's when I hear another roar. A roar I recognise! I open my eyes.

It's my very own tyrannosaurus! He's come back to rescue us!

The tyrannosaurus puts his head down and charges into the giganotosaurus.

For a moment the giganotosaurus is thrown off balance. But he's bigger than the tyrannosaurus. And he's not going to give up his meal that easily. He swipes

his mighty tail at the tyrannosaurus. But the tyrannosaurus ducks and knocks into the giganotosaurus again.

And then he bends down and rests his head on the floor in front of us.

'What's he doing?' shouts Toby.

'I think he wants us to climb onto his back.'

'Are you sure?' says Toby.

The giganotosaurus is back up on its feet. Its mighty jaws are wide open above our heads, ready to gobble us up in one enormous **gulp**.

'Quick,' I shout to Toby, 'climb on!'

I grab Charlie and leap up onto the tyrannosaurus's back. Toby gulps and then follows. Just in time too! The jaws of the giganotosaurus clamp together just behind him.

'Okay, tyrannosaurus,' I shout. 'Run! As fast as you can! To the top of the mountain!'

The tyrannosaurus starts racing back up the rocky slope. He's going really, really *fast*. I have to cling on with all my strength to stop myself falling. The rain is lashing into my eyes and I can hardly see. Squinting, I peer over my shoulder. The giganotosaurus is right behind us!

'Faster, tyrannosaurus, faster!'

We're almost at the top of the mountain. Lightning is flashing in the sky and the thunder is **booming** all around us.

'This is it!' shouts Toby. 'This is the place!'

'Okay,' I shout to the tyrannosaurus, 'put us down!'

The tyrannosaurus leans down and we leap off his back. Toby holds up the time machine and tosses me the **magic** chalk!

'Quick,' he shouts, 'draw a circle.'

As fast as I can I draw a circle around us on the rock. It's not easy in the rain but the chalk still seems to work. It is **magic** chalk, after all. Then Charlie and I join Toby in the centre of the circle.

'Now,' he shouts, 'we need to set the alarms.'

With trembling fingers we set the alarms on the clocks to go off in 60 seconds' time. And then we gather together on an outcrop of rock and wait for lightning to strike.

But we may not have enough time.

The giganotosaurus is coming back to finish his lunch. The tyrannosaurus is standing guard but the giganotosaurus towers above him. He truly is a **monster**. For a few seconds the two enormous carnivores stare at each other. And then they roar and charge! The impact when they meet is incredible. The whole mountain seems to .

At first the tyrannosaurus gets the upper hand. He uses his speed to push the giganotosaurus back. But the giganotosaurus is too strong. With a swipe of his tail he pushes the tyrannosaurus onto his side, and then holds him down with an enormous clawed foot.

'Look at the clouds,' shouts Toby. 'Lightning's going to strike any moment!'

I look up. Crackles of **electricity** are rippling across the swirling clouds above. We're going to make it!

But no! The giganotosaurus has stepped over the tyrannosaurus, and he's racing over towards us. He's too fast. He'll be onto us before the lightning strikes.

The tyrannosaurus is still lying on the ground. He raises his head and lets out another mighty roar. And that's when I see them. Two more tyrannosaurs! Climbing over a rocky rise to our right! I *knew* my tyrannosaurus had friends. The two friends **roar** a reply and race over towards us.

And just in time too!

The giganotosaurus is almost inside the **magic** circle! But at the last moment he looks up. And he knows he's outnumbered! He turns and starts to run back down the mountain, the two new tyrannosaurs hot on his heels!

The crackling in the clouds above us is getting **louder**. The lightning's just about to strike.

I look back at my friend. My friend the tyrannosaurus. He's back on his feet. And he's standing there. Just watching us.

I raise my arm and wave.

'Goodbye tyrannosaurus! Thank you!'

And at the moment I speak the whole sky seems to **explode**. A gigantic fork of lightning shoots out of the clouds and strikes the top of the time machine. Just as the alarms start to go off! The time machine leaps into life and suddenly we're spinning back through the **tunnel** of time.

We're going home!

But just before we disappear I sneak one last look at my tyrannosaurus. And I can't be certain. But I'm fairly sure he winks at me.

CHAPTER 15
home sweet home

We land in my front garden. It's morning, and the street looks normal again. Mr Johnson's car isn't **Crushed**. And Doris Codswallop's fence isn't smashed.

'Where are we?' I ask Toby.

'Yesterday,' he says. 'It's yesterday morning.'

'Yesterday morning?'

'Yes. The day before the tyran-

nosaurus arrived. I set the calculator to turn up one day before we left. To be precise we jumped forward 69 million, 999 thousand, nine hundred and ninety-nine point nine nine years. Which makes it just after 7 am yesterday morning.'

Toby lost me after 69 million. But I'm sure he's right. He usually is.

'Wowee,' says Toby, 'that was a **great** adventure.'

'It certainly was,' I say, 'but I think that's enough time travelling for me.' I look down. I'm still holding Charlie in my arms. 'And for you too, Charlie.'

She woofs in agreement.

'Well,' says Toby, 'I better go home for breakfast.' He gets up. 'I'll probably see you later.'

'Okay,' I say.

Toby walks to the gate.

'Hey Toby,' I call after him.

'Yes?'

'Thanks. I couldn't have done any of it without you.'

Toby smiles. 'My pleasure,' he says. 'Life is certainly never boring having you as a best friend!'

Toby walks out the gate and goes home.

'Well, Charlie,' I say, 'time we went home too.'

I get up and walk into the house. It's three minutes past seven.

'You're late for breakfast,' says Dad.

That night, after everyone has gone to bed, I open my curtains and look outside. It's a clear night. There's a full moon and the sky is filled with stars. I watch the horizon and wait. I know what's about to happen.

And there it is! A shooting star, speeding through the sky.

Now this time I'm going to be sensible. No **silly** wishes for me. The last thing I need is another tyrannosaurus to deal with!

I close my eyes.

And in a very soft voice I whisper, 'I wish for a stegosaurus.'

SAURUS STREET

Saurus Street is just like any other street . . . except for the dinosaurs.

Nick Falk and
Tony Flowers
SAURUS
STREET
An Allosaurus
Ate my Uncle

Nick Falk and
Tony Flowers
SAURUS
STREET
A Plesiosaur
Broke My Bathtub

Nick Falk and
Tony Flowers
SAURUS
STREET
A Diplodocus
Trampled My Teepee

Collect them all!

Watch out for

Billy is a Dragon

by Nick Falk

and Tony Flowers

coming in March 2014